The Mysterious Parcel

FRANCESCA CHESSA

It's a very foggy day. Charlie and Frances are arguing, as usual, about the game they're playing. Suddenly the doorbell rings . . .

'A parcel has come!' shouts Mum.

'It's very big!' yell Charlie and Frances.

'It must be a present for me,' says Charlie. 'It could be a very **big car!**'

'It's not a car,' says Frances. 'It's a speedy scooter for me!'

They both want the parcel so badly that
they start arguing again.

'It's mine!' shouts Frances.

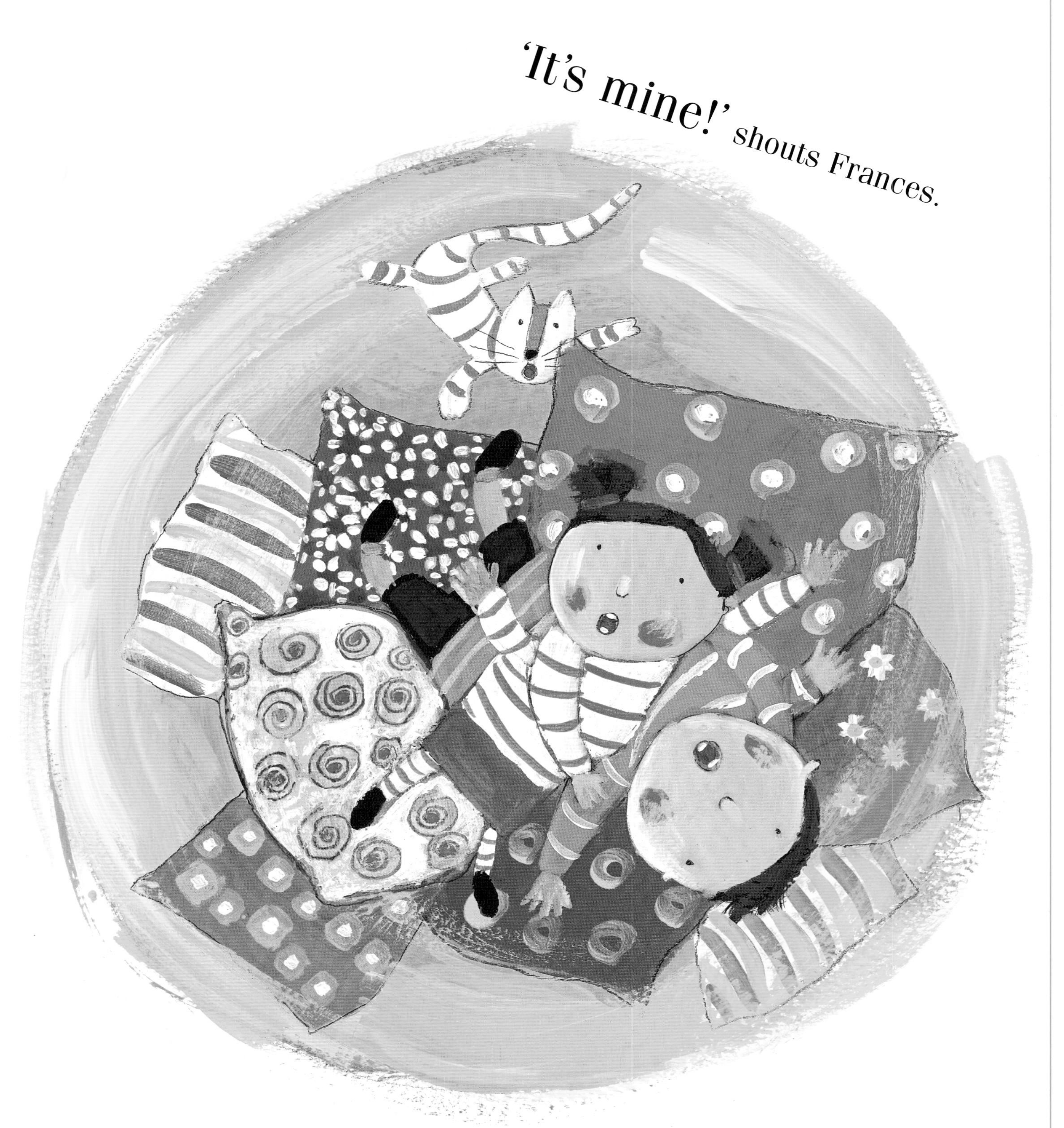

'No, it's mine!' cries Charlie.

‘Mum! Who is that present for?’

they ask together.

‘It’s a surprise,’ says Mum. ‘We have to wait for Daddy to get home before we can open it.’

'If we have to wait for Daddy, then it's definitely something dangerous,' says Charlie. 'Maybe it's a lion!'

'That's impossible, we'd be able to hear him roar!' says Frances.

'But listen!' says Charlie. 'You can hear something like a heartbeat.'

'Yes,' says Frances. 'Maybe the lion isn't roaring because he's fast asleep.'

'If there **IS** a lion in there, then he's **mine**!' says Charlie.

'I'm going to be a brave policeman, and my lion can help me!'

'We will have **SO** much fun together.'

'If there **is** a lion in there, then he's **mine!**' says Frances.

'I'll be fearless
in the night
and we
can sit
and watch the moon
together.'

And they both want the lion so badly that they start arguing again.

'It's mine!' shouts Frances.

'No, it's mine!' cries Charlie.

At last, Daddy comes home.
'Daddy! Please tell us what's inside the parcel,'
ask Charlie and Frances together.

‘But this isn’t my parcel!’ says Daddy. ‘The parcel I’m waiting for is much smaller than this one.’

'Oh no!' think Charlie and Frances.
'Maybe the lion is not for us.'

Just then, the
doorbell rings.

6 Monkey Rd
5 Monkey Rd

It's the courier again. 'I'm sorry, sir. I delivered that parcel to the wrong address this morning. This big parcel was for Mr Red who lives next door – here's **your** parcel.'

'Great!' said Daddy. 'My new tool kit!'

'Hmph! But what can we do with a tool kit?' asks Charlie.

'I know!' says Frances. 'I've got a great idea.'

'Daddy! *We* need *your* tool kit . . .'
they shout together.

'. . . to build a very big house for
the next lion that is delivered!'

And, this time,
Charlie and Frances
don't argue once.

MONKEY Rd.
5